What to doodle?
FANTASTIC FANTASY!

Chuck Whelon

DOVER PUBLICATIONS, INC.
Mineola, New York

Note

Do you ever absentmindedly draw pictures on a piece of scrap paper or the back of a magazine? You may be surprised to find that your doodling leads you to some excellent results! In this exciting book, there are sixty-two pages of ideas for you to use to create your own pictures of wizards, goblins, trolls, princesses, and princes—and much, much more. Drawing has never been more fun, so let's get started on this doodling adventure!

Copyright

Copyright © 2009 by Dover Publications, Inc.
All rights reserved.

Bibliographical Note

What to Doodle? Fantastic Fantasy! is a new work, first published by Dover Publications, Inc., in 2009.

DOVER *Pictorial Archive* SERIES

This book belongs to the Dover Pictorial Archive Series. You may use the designs and illustrations for graphics and crafts applications, free and without special permission, provided that you include no more than four in the same publication or project. (For permission for additional use, please write to Permissions Department, Dover Publications, Inc., 31 East 2nd Street, Mineola, N.Y. 11501.)

However, republication or reproduction of any illustration by any other graphic service, whether it be in a book or in any other design resource, is strictly prohibited.

International Standard Book Number
ISBN-13: 978-0-486-47044-3
ISBN-10: 0-486-47044-X

Manufactured in the United States of America
Dover Publications, Inc., 31 East 2nd Street, Mineola, N.Y. 11501

Wally the Wizard is showing off his new robe.
Decorate it in the most magical way possible!

What is this nasty troll about to bash with his club? Draw a picture of this scary scene.

Design a coat of arms for Sir Montague's shield.

This goblin is about to fall down!
Draw a steed for it to ride on.

**Princess Patty is lost in the forest.
What do you think she sees? Draw it.**

Oh, no! These heroes are about to be attacked.
Show their enemies.

Only one thing is missing from this scene—the commander of the army. Draw this powerful figure.

Simon the Sorcerer loves his magical pet bird.
Draw its picture so Simon can give it a treat.

The witches have called forth the most horrible monster ever seen—and you must draw it!

Show the little creatures that are making life miserable for Buster the Barbarian.

Here's the perfect spot for Lord Henry's new castle. Why don't you draw it for him?

The mythological Centaur is half animal and half man. Now you can finish the picture.

The goblin army needs a picture to decorate
its banner. It's up to you to draw it.

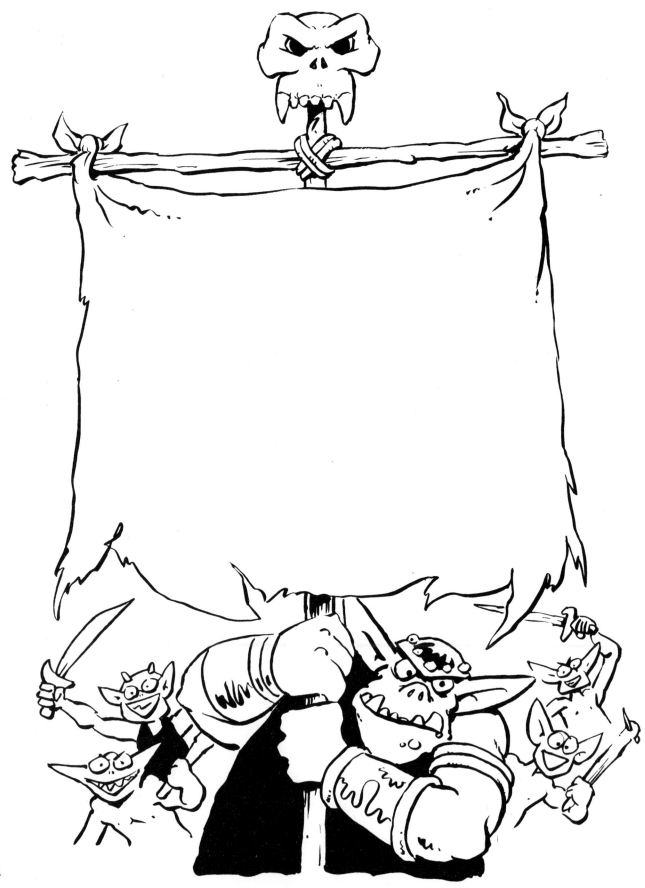

This horseman has discovered a strange building in the desert. Show it.

What is this dragon guarding? Draw its picture.

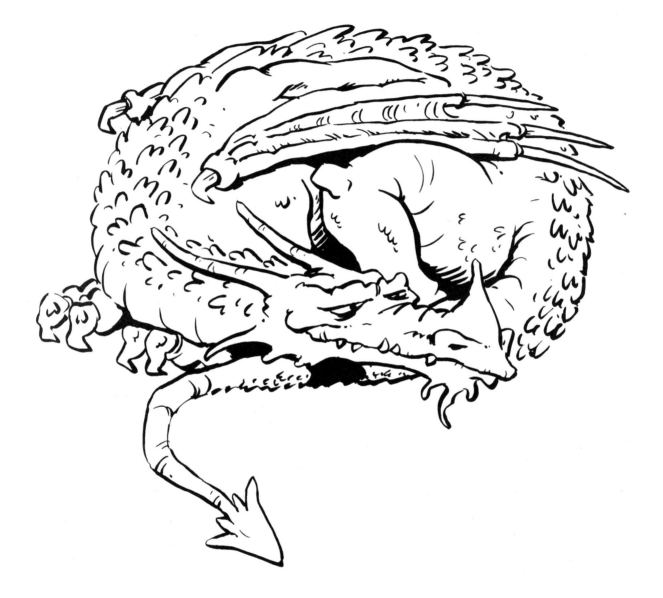

Draw the enemy that this brave soldier meets in the dungeon.

Donald the Dwarf is ready to wield his magical ax.
Draw its picture so that Donald can defend himself.

Draw a couple of elf friends in this tree.

This little sprite is ready to fly off to see her family. Draw a splendid pair of wings for her.

Who is riding on this flying carpet?
Draw a picture so that everyone can see.

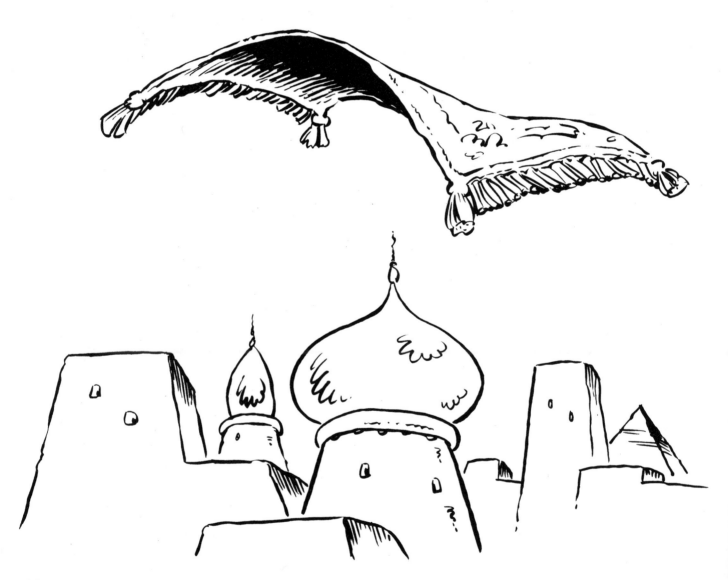

A unicorn lives in this quiet forest. Show what this elegant creature looks like.

The Prince used to be a frog. Draw a picture of what he looks like, now that the evil spell has been broken.

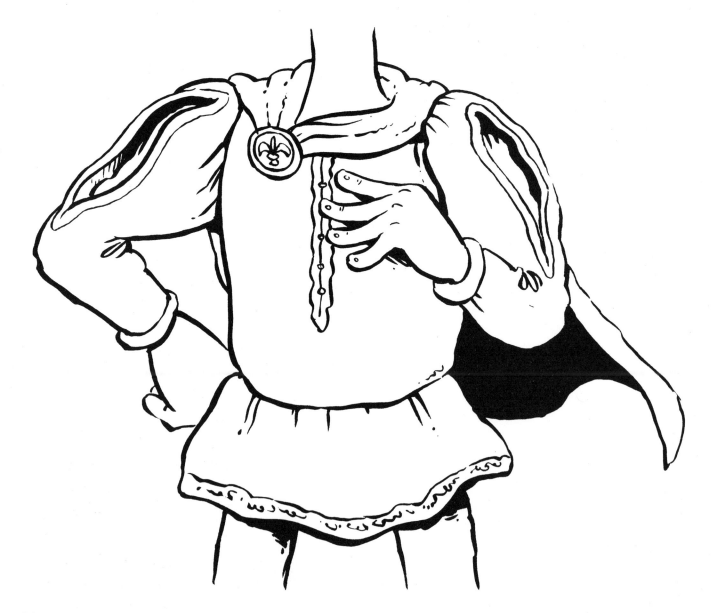

The Dark Overlord demands that a fortress be built for him. It's your task to design it.

What is the great hawk carrying in its claws as it flies over the snow-capped mountains?

What grew out of the ground after Jack planted the magic beans?

Draw the ancient temple that these warriors have discovered.

King Karl can't wait to eat a special feast. Cover
the table with tasty things to eat and drink.

This brave knight deserves a horse, doesn't he? Please draw one for him.

Who is chained to the wall of the castle dungeon?

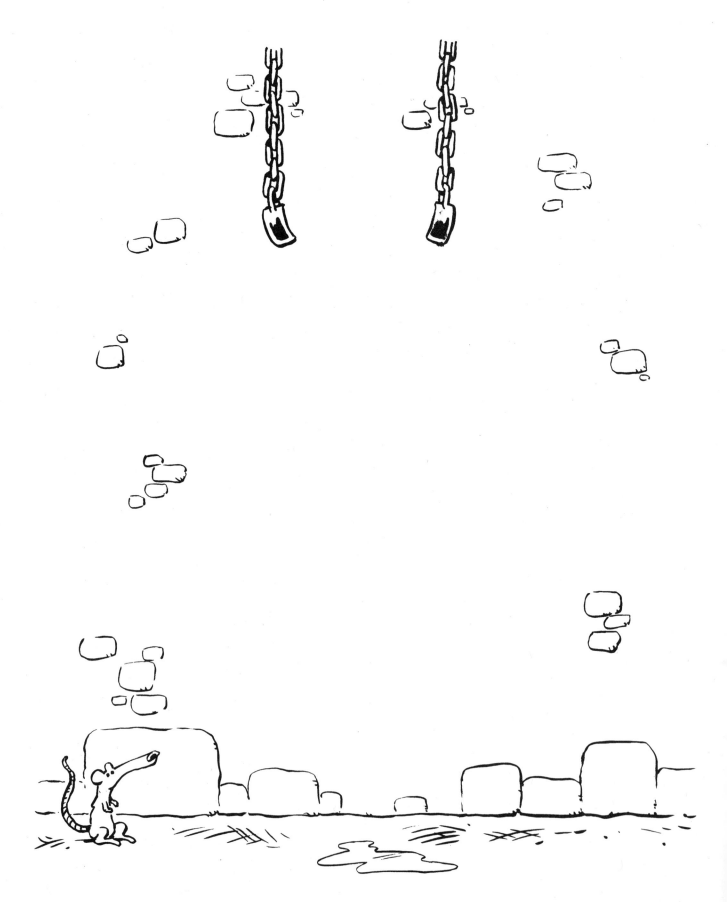

Prince Patrick just spotted a beautiful mermaid in the sea. Draw her picture.

This noble creature demands that you draw a magnificent crown and place it on his head.

A fierce fighter can't wait to join the battle. But first,
you need to draw in the other half of his face!

Won't you design a new outfit for Princess Penny so that she can go to the dress ball?

Draw a picture of the fairy twins that live on this sunflower.

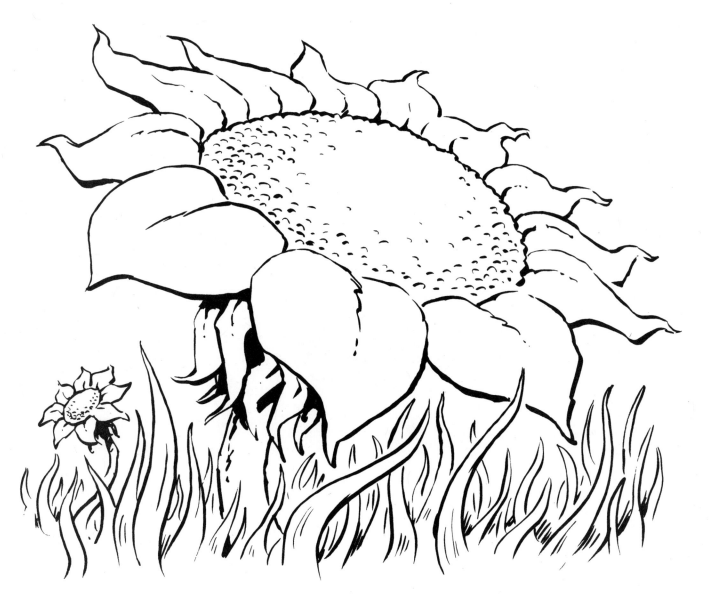

There's a tiny prince in the palm of Princess Frogmilla's hand. Why don't you show what he looks like?

Puss-in-Boots is all dressed up except for his incredibly tall hat. Draw this fantastic headwear.

Someone is about to climb up Rapunzel's hair into the castle. Please draw a picture of this daring individual.

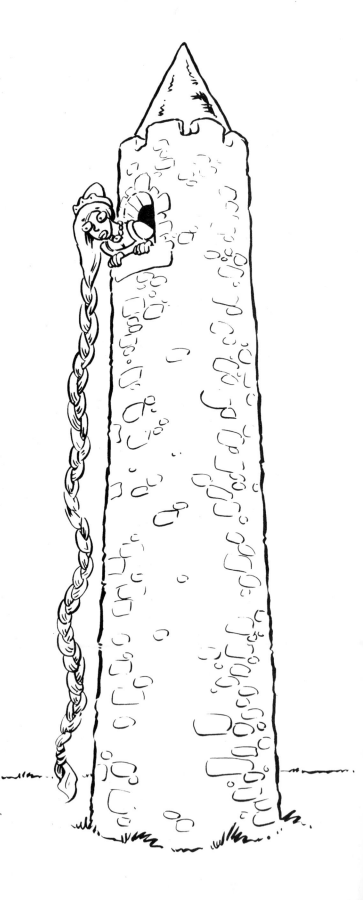

Who (or what) is Sir Belvedere fighting?
You choose—a man or a beast.

Abigail the Archer needs one more thing in order to hit her target. Draw a horse for her to ride on.

Draw a picture of the ice giant that lives in this frozen land.

What horrible creature lives in this swamp? Draw it for all to see.

Mad Meg is up to something wicked.
Draw what is brewing in her cauldron.

Only one person can pull the sword from the stone. Show what he or she looks like.

This tail must belong to something.
What do you think it is?

Many people traveling through town stay at this inn. Your challenge is to draw a sign for it.

**Deep beneath the waves live the mermaids and mermen.
Imagine what life is like under the sea, and then draw it!**

Draw a picture of the great, old tree that stands at the heart of the elves' forest.

This odd-looking creature needs some ears. Decide what they should look like, and then draw them in.

Here is the happy home of an elf family.
Draw them in front of their charming house.

These ancient standing stones are surrounded by spell-casting wizards. Add them to the picture.

**This treasure needs to be guarded against thieves.
Draw a picture to show who will watch over the riches.**

Treeface is lonely. It's been hundreds of years since he had a friend. Draw one for him.

These brave adventurers have turned to stone!
Show who, or what, has carried out this awful deed.

Draw a picture of the fire-breathing dragon that is striking fear into the hearts of the villagers.

Simon the Sorcerer's brother, Stan, is trying
out a new spell. Show what it can do.

Draw a rider for this dragon, and then they will be on their way.

Wilma the Warrior has been ensnared by a hungry plant. Can you draw a picture of it?

Draw a hideous face for this snake-haired Medusa.

Now draw a map of your own fantastic fantasyland!

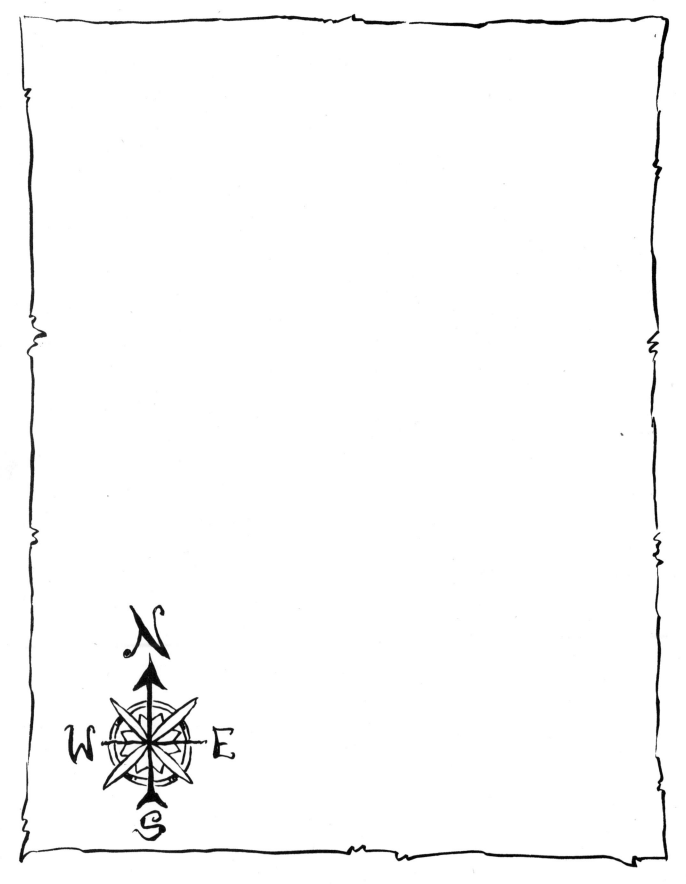